DINOFOURS™

IT'S TIME FOR SCHOOL!

For my mother
— S.M.

Text copyright © 1996 by Scholastic Inc.
Illustrations copyright © 1996 by Hans Wilhelm, Inc.
All rights reserved. Published by Scholastic Inc.
SCHOLASTIC, CARTWHEEL BOOKS, DINOFOURS, and associated logos are trademarks
and/or registered trademarks of Scholastic Inc.

Library of Congress Cataloging-in-Publication Data

Metzger, Steve.
    Dinofours: it's time for school! / by Steve Metzger; illustrated by Hans Wilhelm.
        p.   cm. —(Dinofours)
    Summary: On his first day at preschool, Albert the dinosaur misses his mother, until he makes some new friends
and discovers that school is fun.
    ISBN 0-590-68990-8
    [1. Nursery schools—Fiction. 2. Schools — Fiction. 3. Dinosaurs — Fiction.]
    I. Wilhelm, Hans, 1945- ill. II. Title. III. Series: Metzger, Steve. Dinofours.
PZ7.M56775Di 1996
[E]—dc20   95-49949
                                                                                CIP
                                                                                 AC

        10 9 8 7 6 5 4 3 2 1   03 04 05 06

                        Printed in the U.S.A.   24
                This edition first printing, August 2002

DINOFOURS™

IT'S TIME FOR SCHOOL!

by Steve Metzger
Illustrated by Hans Wilhelm

Cartwheel
·B·O·O·K·S·®

SCHOLASTIC INC.
New York Toronto London Auckland Sydney

It was early September and Albert was going to
school. For the very first time!

"Mommy, will you stay with me at school?"
asked Albert.

"I'll stay for a while," said Albert's mother. "And
then, when you're ready, I'll leave."

"I'll never be ready," said Albert.

Albert and his mother walked inside the school. A friendly dinosaur greeted them.

"Hi, I'm Mrs. Dee. I'm your teacher," she said. "What's your name?"

"Albert," said Albert in a tiny voice.

Albert looked around. He saw children playing in different parts of the classroom. But he didn't know any of them.

"Mommy, please don't go," said Albert. "I'm still not ready."

"Okay," said Albert's mother. "What should we do?"

"Let's play over there," said Albert, pointing to the sand table.

Albert and his mother used shovels and funnels to see which containers held the most sand.

When they filled the last one, Albert's mother said, "Now, it's time for me to go. But before I leave, I'd like you to know something."

Albert's mother sang this song to him:

You're growing up.
It's time for school.
Today's the day you start.
But don't forget, you'll always be
Right inside my heart.

Albert smiled.

"Bye-bye, Albert," said Albert's mother as she walked out of the door.

"Bye-bye, Mommy," said Albert.

All of a sudden, a new boy burst into the classroom.

"Hi, everybody, I'm Brendan!" he shouted. "Wow! Look at all these toys! I'm going to have so much fun. Good-bye, Mom. See you later, alligator."

Albert watched as Brendan quickly made a mud-dough dinosaur.

Then, Brendan skipped over to the blocks area and — lickety-split — built a tall tower with colorful blocks.

Next, he raced over to the easel, where he painted a tree in just a few seconds.

"I'm done," Brendan said. "Now what do I do?"

Mrs. Dee led Brendan to the puzzle table. Albert turned to see what the other children were doing.

Tara was carefully building a firehouse with blocks and pieces of bark. Joshua was looking for his name on the name chart.

And Danielle and Tracy were playing "mommy and baby" in the dress-up area. That made Albert think about his mommy and he began to cry. In a moment, Mrs. Dee was next to him.

"You miss your mommy. Don't you, Albert?" asked Mrs. Dee.

"Yes," sniffled Albert.

"She'll be here later, after our story time," said Mrs. Dee. "But right now I could really use your help. Do you see that doll in the dress-up area? That doll is very sad."

"Why is he sad?" asked Albert, wiping his eyes.

"I don't know," said Mrs. Dee. "Maybe you could ask him."

Albert went over to the dress-up area and asked the doll why he was sad. He held the doll's mouth to his ear so he could hear the answer.

"He said he misses his mommy," said Albert.

"I thought so," said Mrs. Dee. "What do you think would make him feel better?"

"I think he wants to hear a story," said Albert. "Sometimes my mommy reads to me when I'm sad."

"That's a great idea," said Mrs. Dee.

Albert brought the doll to the story corner and showed him all the pictures from *Goldilocks and the Three Bears*. That made Albert feel a little better.

But when Albert heard the sound of crying, he knew someone else was unhappy. Who could it be? He looked over at the puzzle table. It was Brendan.

Albert walked over to the table where Brendan was sitting.

"What's the matter?" asked Albert shyly.

"I miss my mommy," said Brendan. "I'm sad."

"He's sad, too," said Albert, pointing to the doll.

"Maybe he's sad because he wants a toy car," said Brendan as he looked closely at the doll. "He saw one in the store, but his mommy and daddy said he couldn't have it. Let's make him a toy car. Okay?"

"Okay," said Albert.

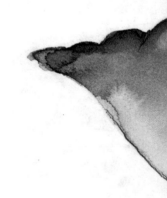

Brendan and Albert built a long car. Then they went to the blocks area and gave the doll lots of rides.

"This is fun," said Albert.

"Yes!" yelled Brendan. "I think he feels a lot better now."

During the rest of that morning's playtime, Albert had a wonderful time with Brendan, his new friend. They especially enjoyed making giant mountains at the sand table.

Later on, Albert met some of the other children.

He and Danielle played a restaurant game in the dress-up area. Danielle was the chef and Albert was the waiter. They served mud-dough cake to their customers.

At snack time, Albert sat next to Tara. He was surprised when Tara tried to take most of the crackers from the basket. Mrs. Dee told her she could only have three.

During outside time, Albert dug for worms with Tracy. And they even found a few! Albert wanted to keep them, but Tracy said they needed to stay in the ground to live.

And at story time, Albert and Joshua giggled at the silly rhymes that Mrs. Dee read.

When Mrs. Dee finished reading, the children turned to face the door. All the parents and baby-sitters were waiting for them.

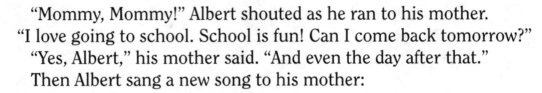

"Mommy, Mommy!" Albert shouted as he ran to his mother. "I love going to school. School is fun! Can I come back tomorrow?"

"Yes, Albert," his mother said. "And even the day after that."

Then Albert sang a new song to his mother:

I'm growing up.
Now I'm in school.
I played and ate my snack.
Mommy, I had fun today,
But now I'm glad you're back.

When he was finished, Albert gave his mother a great, big hug.

DINOFOURS ™

IT'S TIME-OUT TIME!

To Neil Zucker
— S.M.

Library of Congress Cataloging-in-Publication Data

Metzger, Steve.
    It's time-out time! / by Steve Metzger; illustrated by Hans Wilhelm.
       p.   cm. — (Dinofours)
    "Cartwheel books."
    Summary: Because Brendan has a hard time controlling himself with his classmates, his teacher gives him a time-out to
help him think about getting along with others.
    ISBN 0-590-37457-5
    [1. Behavior—Fiction.   2. Nursery schools—Fiction.   3. Schools—Fiction.   4. Dinosaurs—Fiction.]
    I. Wilhelm, Hans, 1945– ill. II. Title. III. Series: Metzger, Steve. Dinofours.
    PZ7.M56775It   1998
  [E]—dc21
                                             97-9117
                                           CIP
                                           AC

DINOFOURS™
IT'S TIME-OUT TIME!

by Steve Metzger
Illustrated by Hans Wilhelm

Cartwheel
·B·O·O·K·S·®

SCHOLASTIC INC.
New York Toronto London Auckland Sydney

It was a busy morning in the Dinofours' classroom.

Brendan was in the blocks area, building a road for his dump truck.

"Left turn!" he said as he made his road go left. "Right turn! Now straight!"

Brendan's road led to Tara, who was constructing a parking garage.

"Get out of the way!" Brendan exclaimed as he put down a long block next to Tara's feet. "Road coming through!"

Tara didn't move. "I'm building a parking garage here," she said.
That made Brendan mad — so mad that he pushed Tara away.
"Hey, stop that!" Tara cried.
"You're in my way!" shouted Brendan.
In an instant, Mrs. Dee arrived.

"I see two children who are very upset," she said. "What's going on here?"

"Brendan pushed me," Tara said. "He said I was in his way."

"There's plenty of room in the blocks area for both of you," Mrs. Dee said. "And Brendan, you know that pushing is not the way we settle arguments."

Mrs. Dee put her arms around Tara and Brendan.

"Tara, how did you feel when Brendan pushed you?" she asked.

"Mad!" said Tara.

"I'd like you to tell that to Brendan," Mrs. Dee said.

Brendan put his hands over his ears.

"Brendan," said Mrs. Dee. "You need to hear what Tara has to say. Please put your hands down."

"Oh, all right," he said, lowering his hands.

"Brendan," Tara said, "it makes me mad when you push me."

"Okay, Tara," Mrs. Dee said. "I want to talk to Brendan alone now." Tara went back to her parking garage. Mrs. Dee turned to Brendan.

"Remember," she said. "We use our words to solve problems at school."

"Okay," said Brendan.

As Mrs. Dee looked to see what the other children were doing, Brendan walked over to the art table. Tracy and Danielle were drawing pictures with markers.

Brendan started to draw a volcano. He wanted a red marker, and Tracy had one.

"Tracy," Brendan said. "I need your red marker to make lava for my volcano."

"I'm using it now," said Tracy. "I'll give it to you when I'm done."

Brendan forgot what Mrs. Dee said about using his words to solve problems.

"I want it, now!" Brendan said as he grabbed Tracy's marker, making a long line across her picture.

"Mrs. Dee!" Tracy cried out. "Brendan made a line on my kitty. He ruined it."

Mrs. Dee walked quickly to the art table. First, she comforted Tracy. Then she turned to Brendan.

"Brendan, I see that you're not able to be with the other children right now," she said. "You need a time-out."

"But I don't want a time-out," Brendan said.

"I know you don't," said Mrs. Dee. "But you're having a hard time controlling yourself."

Mrs. Dee took one of the chairs from the art table and placed it on the rug.

Brendan sat down. Then he sang this song to Mrs. Dee:

I do not want to sit here.
I only want to play.
This time-out really makes me mad.
Do I have to stay?

"Yes, you do," said Mrs. Dee. "For about three minutes."
Mrs. Dee turned as she heard her name called. Another child needed help in a different part of the classroom.
"I'll be back soon," Mrs. Dee said, leaving for the book corner.

When Mrs. Dee left, Brendan began to dance and make silly faces.
"Look at me," he said. "I'm a funny clown."
Mrs. Dee came right back.

"Sit down, Brendan," Mrs. Dee said. "This is not a time for silliness."

Brendan sat down.

"I want you to think about what you've been doing this morning," Mrs. Dee said.

"Okay," he said, looking down at the floor.

Brendan remembered making the line on Tracy's picture and how he had pushed Tara.

I wouldn't like them doing that to me, he thought.

After a few moments, Mrs. Dee spoke to Brendan again.

"Take a look over there," she said, pointing to Tracy and Danielle. "Do you see how well they're playing together?"

Brendan nodded.

"Now, please look at the science table," Mrs. Dee said.

Albert and Tara were laughing as they put twigs and rocks on a scale.

"I see Albert and Tara playing together," Brendan said. "And they're having fun."

"Yes," said Mrs. Dee. "I think you can play cooperatively with other children, too. Your time-out is over now."

Brendan bounced out of his chair and went right to the puzzle shelf. He looked for the jungle puzzle. That was his favorite.

Where is it? he wondered.

At that moment, Brendan saw Joshua playing with the jungle puzzle. Brendan was just about to grab the puzzle away — but he stopped himself.

Brendan looked around the classroom and saw the other children playing together.

"Joshua, can I help you with the jungle puzzle?" Brendan asked. "I know where the gorilla goes."

"Sure," Joshua said.

Working as a team, Brendan and Joshua put all the pieces of the jungle puzzle together.

When they finished, Mrs. Dee walked over.

"I just saw what happened," said Mrs. Dee. "Brendan, you should be proud of yourself. I'm proud of you, too."

Brendan smiled.

Then he sang a new song:

I stopped myself! I stopped myself!
I did it, Mrs. Dee.
I didn't take the puzzle.
I'm glad you're proud of me.

Afterward, Brendan found Tara. He asked her if he could connect his road to Tara's parking garage.

And she agreed.

DINOFOURS™

MY SEEDS WON'T GROW!

To Aunt Joyce
— S.M.

Text copyright © 2000 by Scholastic Inc.
Illustrations copyright © 2000 by Hans Wilhelm, Inc.
All rights reserved. Published by Scholastic Inc.
SCHOLASTIC, CARTWHEEL BOOKS, DINOFOURS, and associated logos are trademarks
and/or registered trademarks of Scholastic Inc.

Library of Congress Cataloging-in-Publication Data

Metzger, Steve.
   Dinofours: my seeds won't grow! / by Steve Metzger; illustrated by Hans Wilhelm.
      p.   cm. — (Dinofours)
"Cartwheel books."
   Summary: Upset that the plants he is growing are the smallest in the class, four-year-old dinosaur Brendan
switches his name to another container but then regrets what he has done.
   ISBN 0-439-06329-9
   [1. Plants — Fiction. 2. Schools — Fiction. 3. Dinosaurs — Fiction.
4. Honesty — Fiction.] I. Wilhelm, Hans, 1945- ill. II. Title.
III. Title: My Seeds Won't Grow. IV. Series: Metzger, Steve. Dinofours.
PZ7.M56775Dj 2000
   [E]—dc21

                                                             99-15530
                                                                 CIP

DINOFOURS™

MY SEEDS WON'T GROW!

by Steve Metzger
Illustrated by Hans Wilhelm

Cartwheel
·B·O·O·K·S·®

SCHOLASTIC INC.
New York   Toronto   London   Auckland   Sydney
Mexico City   New Delhi   Hong Kong

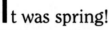t was spring!

Mrs. Dee gathered the children around the science table.

"We're going to plant green bean seeds today," she said. "What do you think these seeds need to grow?"

"Dirt from the plant store," Danielle said.

"Yes," said Mrs. Dee. "It's also called soil. Anything else?"

"Water!" Joshua added.

"Sunshine, too!" said Tracy.

"My, my," said Mrs. Dee. "You know a lot about seeds. Now, how do you think they'll change?"

"Maybe they'll grow into a tall beanstalk, like the one in *Jack and the Beanstalk*," Albert said. "That's a scary story with a giant."

"I really don't think that will happen," said Mrs. Dee. "Any other ideas?"

"These are green bean seeds," said Tara. "So they'll grow into green bean plants."

"Let's plant the seeds now!" Brendan said excitedly. "I can't wait to see mine grow. They'll be the biggest in the whole class!"

"No, they won't!" said Tara.

"Yes, they will!" said Brendan. "You'll see."

"All right, children," said Mrs. Dee. "Let's begin."

Mrs. Dee gave each child three green bean seeds, some soil, a small container for planting, a spoon, and a measuring cup with water in it.

The children planted the seeds and watered them. Then, Mrs. Dee passed out craft sticks with their names on them to put in their containers.

"It's time to pick your next activity," Mrs. Dee announced. All the children left the table—except Brendan.

"I think I'll sit here and watch my seeds grow into plants," he said. Then, Brendan sang this song:

My seeds will grow and grow and grow—
So very big and tall.
They'll grow and grow until they are
The biggest plants of all!

"Brendan, it takes a while for seeds to grow," Mrs. Dee said.
"Okay," Brendan said as he walked away. "But I'll be back to check on them later."

For the next few days Brendan was the first child to arrive at school.
He ran right to the windowsill where the seed containers were placed.
It was always the same—nothing was growing.

"My seeds won't grow!" he said. "What's wrong?"

"There's nothing wrong," Mrs. Dee said. "You just need to be patient, that's all."

Brendan noticed that his soil was dry, so he added some water.

"Maybe tomorrow they'll grow," he said.

Two weeks passed and still no plants. That Friday afternoon, Mrs. Dee gathered the Dinofours to say good-bye for the weekend.

"I know everyone is hoping our green bean seeds will grow soon," she said.

"Especially me," said Brendan.

"Yes," said Mrs. Dee, "especially Brendan. Perhaps we'll see some changes on Monday morning."

"I hope so," said Brendan.

"And don't forget," Mrs. Dee said. "Monday is Danielle's birthday. We're going to have a class party to celebrate."

Everybody cheered. Then, Mrs. Dee dismissed the children to their parents, grandparents, and babysitters.

On Monday morning, Brendan was the first to arrive—as usual. He ran to the seed containers.

At first, Brendan was happy to see that all the children's seeds had sprouted. But when he compared his container with the others, his mood quickly changed.

My plants are the smallest, he said to himself. *And Joshua's are the biggest. How could that be?*

Making sure that no one was looking, Brendan switched his name stick with Joshua's. Now he had the tallest plants and Joshua had the smallest.

As the other children arrived, Brendan showed them how the seeds had grown.

"See, I told you I would have the tallest plants," he said.

Joshua saw that he had the smallest plants. Instead of getting upset, he shrugged his shoulders and walked away.

Later that day, the children gathered at the snack table for Danielle's birthday party.

"We're having blueberry muffins," Danielle said, pointing to the basket Mrs. Dee was holding. "My mommy and I baked them last night."

Mrs. Dee gave each child a muffin. Brendan noticed that the blueberries on his muffin made a face with a big smile.

"Look!" Brendan said to Tracy. "My muffin has a happy face. It's special."

Tracy looked at Brendan's muffin, then back at her own.

My muffin is so plain, she thought. *It's not special, like Brendan's.*

As the children turned their heads to sing "Happy Birthday" to Danielle, Tracy switched her muffin with Brendan's.

When Brendan saw what Tracy had done, he said, "You took my muffin. Give it back!"

"I'm Danielle's best friend," Tracy said. "I should have the special muffin!"

"No fair!" Brendan shouted. "That muffin is mine!"

Then, Brendan remembered how he had switched his name stick with Joshua's.

That wasn't fair either, he said to himself.

"Mrs. Dee," Brendan said. "I have something to tell you."

Mrs. Dee walked over to Brendan.

"This morning I saw that Joshua's plants were the biggest and mine were the smallest," he said. "I was sad, so I switched our names. I'm sorry."

"Brendan," Mrs. Dee replied.
"I'm a little disappointed about what you did. But I'm very pleased to see how honest you are. Now let's talk to Joshua."

Brendan apologized to Joshua and sang this song to him:

When I switched our names today,
I hoped you wouldn't care.
But now I see
How bad it feels,
When things are so unfair.

"But now my plants are the smallest ones in the class," Brendan said. "I'm still sad about that."

"Maybe they'll catch up later," Joshua said.

And after a while, that's just what happened.

DINOFOURS™

IT'S CLASS TRIP DAY!

To Mutti
— S.M.

Text copyright © 1997 by Scholastic Inc.
Illustrations copyright © 1997 by Hans Wilhelm, Inc.
All rights reserved. Published by Scholastic Inc.
SCHOLASTIC, CARTWHEEL BOOKS, DINOFOURS, and associated logos are trademarks
and/or registered trademarks of Scholastic Inc.

Library of Congress Cataloging-in-Publication Data
Metzger, Steve.
    Dinofours: it's class trip day! / by Steve Metzger; illustrated by Hans Wilhelm.
    p.   cm.— (Dinofours)
    Summary: Tara does not want to go on the class field trip to Dino Pond, but when she saves a nest of baby birds
she decides that field trips are not so bad after all.
    ISBN 0-590-68993-2
    [1. School field trips—Fiction. 2. Nursery schools—Fiction. 3. Schools—Fiction. 4. Dinosaurs—Fiction.]
    I. Wilhelm, Hans, 1945- ill. II. Title. III. Series: Metzger, Steve. Dinofours.
PZ7.M56775Dhf   1997
[E]—dc20
                                                                                                      95-53229
                                                                                                          CIP
                                                                                                           AC

DINOFOURS™
IT'S CLASS TRIP DAY!

by Steve Metzger
Illustrated by Hans Wilhelm

Cartwheel
B·O·O·K·S ®

SCHOLASTIC INC.
New York Toronto London Auckland Sydney

Today was class trip day!
    Mrs. Dee called the children over to the big rug in the corner of their classroom.
    "Okay," she began. "Please make a circle."

The children quickly looked for places to sit on the rug.

"Brendan, you're too close," Tara said. "You're sitting on my leg."

"There's no room," Brendan said as he pushed Tara away. "You have to move over."

"All right, children," said Mrs. Dee. "Why don't we all move back a little and we'll have a bigger circle?"

The children moved back.

"That's better," said Mrs. Dee. "Now, who knows what we're going to do today?"

All the children raised their hands. Mrs. Dee called on Tracy.

"We're going to walk through the woods to Dino Pond," she said.

"And we're going to see ducks and frogs!" Joshua shouted.

"And the biggest tree in the whole world!" said Danielle in a clear, loud voice.

"Yes, Danielle," said Mrs. Dee. "Some dinosaurs think the old oak tree next to Dino Pond is the biggest tree in the world."

"It is," said Albert softly. "My daddy told me so."

"Mrs. Dee! Mrs. Dee!" Brendan called out. "Will we eat lunch there, too? My mommy made me three peanut butter and jelly sandwiches."

"Yes," Mrs. Dee said, smiling to herself. "We'll eat our lunches after we arrive at Dino Pond."

Then, Mrs. Dee noticed that Tara's head was down.

"Tara, you've been very quiet this morning," said Mrs. Dee. "What do you think we'll see at Dino Pond?"

"I don't care what we see!" said Tara. "I don't want to go!"

"Why not?" asked Mrs. Dee.

"It's too hot. There are too many bugs. And we're not going to have a story time because of this silly trip."

"I might be able to tell a story if we get back early," Mrs. Dee replied. "And, who knows? Perhaps you'll have some fun."

"I won't!" said Tara.

"Well, we'll see," said Mrs. Dee as she glanced at the clock. "Looks like it's time for us to go. Danielle, it's your turn to be the line leader today."

"Great! I'll pick Tracy to be my partner," said Danielle.

Mrs. Dee helped the other children find partners as they lined up at the door. Tara wanted to be with Joshua, but he was already Albert's partner. The only child left was Brendan. And Tara didn't want to be *his* partner. Today's class trip was getting worse, not better.

"Let's remember the safety rules," said Mrs. Dee as she gathered the lunches in a shopping bag. "You must always hold hands with your partner. And you must never, *ever,* walk away from the group."

The children walked past their playground and on to the path that led to Dino Pond.

"While we're walking," said Mrs. Dee, "I want you to be nature scientists. Use your ears to listen and eyes to see."

"All I see are mosquitoes," said Tara, "and I hate them."

"Does anyone see anything else?" asked Mrs. Dee.

"I see flowers," said Joshua.

"And I see lots of white clouds," said Tracy.

"Wonderful," said Mrs. Dee. "Does anyone hear anything?"

"I hear sticks crunching under my feet," said Danielle.

"And I hear something growling," said Brendan. "I think it's my stomach. Is it time for lunch yet, Mrs. Dee?"

"No, Brendan," answered Mrs. Dee. "We'll have lunch later on. Please try to be patient."

Tara began to sing a song:

I hate this trip.
It's hot and here's a bug.
Let's go back to school—
For stories on the rug.

After walking a while longer, the Dino Pond came into view.
"We're here!" Tracy shouted.

The children cheered. Except for Tara.
"Is it time to eat?" asked Brendan.
"Not yet," replied Mrs. Dee.
The children walked over to the edge of Dino Pond and looked into the water. They happily pointed out frogs and turtles to one another. Except for Tara.

"Now, let's take a look at the top of the old oak tree," said Mrs. Dee.

If everybody is looking up, thought Tara, *I'm going to look down.*

As she did, Tara noticed something moving on the ground. Walking closer, she heard chirping sounds. It was a bird's nest! With three baby birds!

The rest of the children were still looking up at the old
oak tree.

"It has a hole in it," said Joshua.

"Maybe a squirrel lives inside," said Danielle.

"I can't see the hole in the tree," said Albert. "There's a
branch in the way."

"If everyone moves back a few steps," said Mrs. Dee,
"we can all see."

The children began moving backward.
"Stop!" yelled Tara in her loudest voice.

Mrs. Dee walked over.

"What's going on?" she asked.

"There's a bird's nest on the ground," Tara said. "With baby birds. I yelled because I didn't want them to get hurt."

"Look at that!" exclaimed Mrs. Dee. "Tara's right. How did you know they were here?"

"I saw something moving on the ground," said Tara. "Then I heard chirping sounds."

"Tara," said Mrs. Dee, "you used your eyes to see and your ears to hear. You're a real nature scientist."

Tara smiled her biggest smile in a long time.

The children gathered around the bird's nest to get a closer look at the baby birds.

"Please, don't get too close," said Mrs. Dee. "We don't want to frighten them."

"The nest probably fell from a branch," said Joshua.

"Yes," said Mrs. Dee. "And because you found the nest, Tara, you get to put it back in the tree. I'll lift you up. Please be careful not to touch the baby birds."

Mrs. Dee helped Tara place the bird's nest on the branch above them.

"Where's the mommy bird?" asked Albert.

"I don't know," said Mrs. Dee. "But I hope she comes back soon. The baby birds are probably hungry."

"Me, too," said Brendan.

"She'll come back," said Tara. "I know she will."

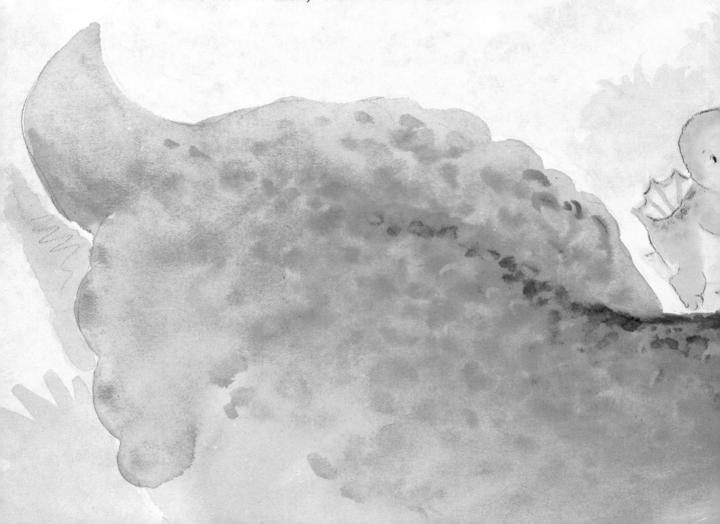

Just then, the mother bird flew back to the bird's nest. After checking on her babies, she flew around Tara's head, chirping loudly.

"I think she's saying 'Thank you' to Tara," Joshua said.

"Yes," said Tara. "She's saying, 'Thank you very much.'"

"Tara," said Mrs. Dee, "when we get back to school, I think we'll have enough time for one new story. Do you have any idea what that story might be?"

"No, I don't, Mrs. Dee," said Tara.

"*How Tara Saved the Baby Birds*," said Mrs. Dee.

The children cheered.

Just then, Brendan walked up to Mrs. Dee.
"Can we eat now?" asked Brendan.
Mrs. Dee looked at the others.
"What do you think?" she asked. "Is it time for lunch?"
They all said "yes" together!

On their way home, Tara sang a happy, new song:

I found the nest,
Sitting on the ground.
Now it's in the tree.
The birds are safe and sound.